Murder by Marina

MOON'S LANDING COZY MYSTERY SERIES
BOOK TWO

SHELLEY WEISS

Murder by Marina

Chapter One

"There's been a murder," Blanche whispered as she parked the car outside of the marina. "Do you have your camera ready? We won't have long before the sheriff arrives." She removed a voice recorder from her purse. Blanche's a reporter for the local newspaper, Moon's News, and I'm the photographer. "We don't know what we're walking into," she said. "But I'll need you to be ready."

"A murder?" I asked as I removed my camera from its bag. "What exactly are we doing here?"

Blanche had been at my home when she received a mysterious text urging her to get to the marina A.S.A.P. She stepped out of the car and motioned for me to follow. *Just what are we doing here?* I should have asked more questions before agreeing to this late-night outing with my Coon Hound, Butterscotch. But Blanche's excitement rubbed off on me, and we left in a hurry.

"Blanche, wait." I hurried out of the car to catch up with her.

She had her phone in her hand and sent a quick text before returning to me. "Hurry, it's this way!" She was using her phone as a guide, as though she were tracking someone's location.

Butterscotch, ever eager to explore unfamiliar scents around her, wasted no time tugging at her leash as she hurried after Blanche. "Hold on," I cried in panic, fearing I'd lose hold of the leash.

Blanche waved at me to hurry. "I got a tip that something happened at the marina," she whispered.

I noticed several yachts docked for the night but didn't see anything unusual. Moon's Landing is a popular tourist destination nestled in Northern California, and usually, the docks would be a busy place, even at this hour, but not tonight.

I had only recently moved back to town after inheriting my aunt's dog, Butterscotch, and her Victorian Manor. Before I could settle into my life here in Moon's Landing, my old friend Blanche Pruitt had hired me as a photographer for her father's newspaper. It's an excellent opportunity to work with my friend again and have a flexible job, so I didn't hesitate when I said yes.

Blanche's phone pinged, alerting her to a text message. She read it and pocketed her phone. "It doesn't look like the police are here — yet! But we've got to move fast — this way!"

"Blanche, wait," I said, grabbing her arm and keeping her from taking another step. I wanted answers. "What's going on? Who are you texting?" Butterscotch pulled at the leash, eager to investigate a scent she had picked up.

"It's simple. You're a photographer, and I need you to take photos. Don't worry, you'll see in a second. It's this way." She darted down the dock and headed to the left. I followed her as she weaved around the marina.

"I get the idea that there's a story here," I said, hurrying to catch up to her. "But a murder?" I expected to hear emergency sirens, but I didn't. How is it that Blanche knew about this murder? And who told her about it?

I didn't have to wait much longer. As we approached a fishing vessel, I found my answer: there was something significant tangled up in the nets. "What is that?" I asked, standing at her side in confusion. "Is that..."

"Get to work," she urged. "Just don't step in anything. I'm—"

"Blanche," I interrupted.

"There he is. I'm going to interview that man." She took out her recorder and some cash. "Thanks for the tip."

"I saw your ad in the newspaper about dialing in tips," he said as he counted the money. "Glad to see you pay well."

"Blanche," I said firmly as I pointed at the net. "Is that a body?"

She nodded. "Just don't step in any of the evidence." She remarked casually. Just how many crime scenes has she been to?

I took a photo of the man she was standing next to. He didn't seem to notice as he was busy speaking with Blanche. He was dressed in an old pair of jeans with patches, and his coat was zipped up to his neck to ward off frigid sea air. I tugged at my jacket as I suddenly felt chilled.

Blanche wanted me to photograph the crime scene, but we were out of here as soon as I was done. I returned my camera to the body caught in the fishing nets and zoomed in with my lens... wait... I know him!

A light breeze brushed my hair against the lens, ruining the shot. Butterscotch began barking; she didn't like the scent she picked up on the wind, and I didn't blame her.

I recognized the body... I had met him once before. His name was Nick Baker.

A lobster jumped onto a crate beside me, startling me and causing Butterscotch to bark. She nearly broke free of the leash as she tugged to chase after the lobster, who ran down the dock and to the boat.

"Butterscotch, let it go. We got work to do."

The whirl of emergency sirens rang in the distance. A woman screamed over my shoulder, causing me to drop the leash. Butterscotch reared free and ran after the lobster who had boarded the boat.

I ran after her, calling her name, but she was determined to catch that lobster.

"Birdie," Blanche shouted. "What are you doing?"

Chapter Two

BUTTERSCOTCH CAME TO A HALT AND TURNED, AND to my dismay, she had the lobster in her mouth. "Let go of that," I ordered. She promptly listened. The lobster jumped off the boat and splashed into the water.

Blanche rushed over with a panicked look in her green eyes. "What are you two doing? Get off the *Ecstatic* — it's a crime scene!"

"That's Nick Baker," I shouted to Blanche, pointing at the body tangled in the nets.

"Nick Baker?" She asked as she boarded the boat. "How are you so sure?"

I turned my back to Nick, my eyes sharp on Blanche. "I talked to him at Peter Hayes's garage. We have to get off this boat." I grabbed Butterscotch's leash and hurried off the ship but froze.

"Birdie?"

Peter Hayes was calmly standing beside the fisherman Blanche had been interviewing, lighting a cigarette.

"What's Peter doing here?"

"He has a boat in the marina," Blanche explained. "Let's go talk to him."

Peter began to walk away but stopped as Blanche shouted his name. The dock quickly filled up as those who called it home were waking up.

Butterscotch sniffed at his hand as we reached him. He leaned down to pet her, but she moved away. "What are you doing here?" He asked as he rose to his feet. "Did I hear you say that's Baker in there?"

Blanche positioned herself in front of me as she began to question him. "When was the last time you saw Nick?" she asked. "Did you ask him to come down here?" She raised the recorder to his face, causing him to step back.

"I haven't seen Peter since he left the shop," he said, flicking ashes onto the dock. "Are you sure that's him?" He pointed over her shoulder.

The sirens grew closer, causing Blanche to press him harder. "But he could have been here to see you."

I snapped a photo of them speaking, causing Peter to wince in protest. "Don't take my photo," he snapped.

Deputy Lomack was the first to arrive. He raised his hand and pointed at us in accusation. "What is going on here?" he shouted. "What are any of you doing here?" His salt-and-pepper hair was pressed on one side of his head like he had been awakened from a deep sleep.

Blanche hurried over to Lomack, her recorder held close to his face. "The body of Nick Baker has been found. What can you tell us about it, Deputy Lomack?"

His gaze was sharp and direct as he pointed to the other side of the docks. "You and the rest of your friends can stand there and out of my crime scene. How did you even hear about this?" His eyes moved across us until they settled on Butterscotch. "Is that a dog in my crime scene?" He ran a hand through his hair. "Get it out of here."

"No need to tell us twice." Blanche lowered her recorder. "How about off the record?"

"I'm not going to bite, and I won't repeat myself, but I'll be happy to put you and your friends in a cell for the night for obstruction."

Blanche moved back to me and grabbed my arm. My camera strap caught on my earring as she jerked me out of the way. I couldn't hear what she mumbled. But I noticed Peter Hayes slipping away before Lomack and Deputy Murphy had a chance to speak with him. The docks began filling up with even more curious onlookers who heard all the noise.

I tugged at my ear and noticed my earring was missing. "Oh no," I gasped. "My earring must have fallen off."

"Lomack can protest all he wants, but he's not chasing us out of here," Blanche remarked, oblivious to my distress. Butterscotch set her eyes on Blanche with concern and understanding. She was so good at sensing one's emotions. "I need to get back in there and speak with witnesses," Blanche said, determined. I knew her well enough to know there would be no stopping her.

"Lomack was clear," I reminded. "He doesn't want us in his crime scene, and I don't want to get arrested on my first day working for you."

She whirled away from me as though she were looking at a stage, not a crime scene. "This is a big story! And my newspaper could use the increased readership. I have to get back in there."

"How are we going to do that without Lomack seeing us?" I asked.

Blanche raised her eyebrows as she pointed at my camera. "Birdie, start taking photos. Try to get as much as you can. I will see who I can find that will talk with me."

"You want me to take photos?"

"That's what I'm paying you for." She tapped my camera.

"I'm going to see if Deputy Murphy's here. He might talk to me." She moved away, weaving through the crowd.

"Blanche!" I shouted, but she didn't stop. I tugged my earlobe again and brushed my hand through my hair, hoping the earring had gotten caught up in my hair and had not fallen to the ground.

No such luck.

Butterscotch stood, her ears raised as she waited for me to decide what to do. "Let's get to work," I said to her. She barked and wagged her tail, eager.

I snapped a few photos, trying to tell a story with pictures. I had little experience as a photographic journalist but knew how to tell a story with images. I took a step back as I looked around me with my camera in my hands. Holding it to my eye, I studied my surroundings through my lens.

"Umph," I muttered as my shoulder was bumped from behind. I nearly lost my camera.

"Excuse me," a male voice said in my ear. I turned to see who apologized, but I only saw the back of his grey hooded sweatshirt as he moved through the crowd.

My bag felt heavier, but I thought little about it as I returned to work. If only I had been more observant of what had just happened. It might have saved me a lot of trouble...

Chapter Three

Blanche and I stayed until the Coroner had removed the body. We had overheard the deputies looking for a knife. They believe one was used in the murder. It was nearly six a.m. as Blanche dropped Butterscotch and me at home.

"I'll need your photos, A.S.A.P.," Blanche stated firmly. "Can you put them on a flash drive? I can wait."

"Why don't you come in? I'll make us some coffee," I suggested as Butterscotch barked impatiently at me for my attention. "And yes, I'll get your breakfast ready, too."

Butterscotch raced me up the stairs, eager for her breakfast.

"Just give me a minute while I get her fed," I said as Blanche followed us.

She dropped her oversized bag on the kitchen table and slumped into a chair. "This is such a mess," she cried.

"What's wrong?" I asked, reaching for her shoulder, concerned. "You did great at the marina." I thought maybe Blanche could use some reassurance on what a great job she did.

She reached into her bag to remove a tissue and began dabbing her eyes. "I haven't told you something," she mumbled.

"What haven't you told me?" I couldn't imagine what it could be.

She tossed her tissue inside her bag and rested her chin on the back of her hand in defeat before suddenly sitting up. "Can I use your bathroom?"

"Sure, I'll get the coffee started."

She hurried out of the kitchen, and I made Butterscotch her breakfast. When I had the instant coffee ready, Blanche returned to the kitchen.

"It's my dad," she said with concern as she sat. "He hasn't been well."

This news was new to me. I've known Fred Pruitt for as long as I've known Blanche. He loved magic and always had a new magic trick to show me.

I joined her at the island table and placed a coffee before her. "What's wrong with him?" I asked.

"He's on hospice," she said solemnly. "I've been covering for him at the paper. You know how much that place means to him. But over the years, subscriptions have dwindled. We are on the brink of closing our doors, and I can't let him see that happen."

"Blanche, I'm so sorry," I hugged her as she cried. "What can I do?" I asked as she calmed. "Can I help him in any way? Or you?"

She nodded. "You can keep this between us. Outside of his doctor and in-home nurse, no one knows what's happening, and I'd prefer to keep it this way. At least for now."

"That's why you pushed so hard at the crime scene." I began to understand why she was insistent. "I can get you the photos, but it'll take me at least an hour to go through and pick out the best ones."

She sighed heavily. "That would be too late; I need them now. I don't want someone else to scoop this story." She reached for my laptop, which was left on the island table. "I'm going to log you into our website. You can upload the photos directly." She began typing in the address. "Can I borrow this? I need to work on the article."

I retrieved my camera bag from the side table I had dropped it on, and as I reached in to remove my camera to review my photos, my hand grazed something sharp. I pulled my hand back and brought my stinging fingers to my mouth to soothe them.

Opening the bag wider, I gasped in shock. "Blanche," I shouted. "Blanche!"

She rushed to my side. "What is it? You sound as though you are fighting for your life!"

I didn't want to take it out to show her; I was too afraid to touch it. "Look inside my bag," I ordered as I reached for my cell phone to call the Sheriff's Station.

Carefully, she approached my bag. "I'm not sure I want to," she whispered.

"Just look!"

She peeked into the bag and then lurched back in shock. Her face was draining of color. "How did that get in your bag?"

A knock sounded at my door. "Ms. Lopez?" Lomack's familiar voice called my name.

"Is this what I think it is?" Blanche whispered.

"I don't know — but what is it doing in my bag?"

"Hide this." Blanche quickly shut my camera bag and tucked it inside a cabinet. "Don't you dare tell him about what's inside—"

"But I have to — I can't hide this. We need to turn this in. It could be evidence."

"You have every reason to hide this." She firmly clamped her hand onto my arm. "Not a word, promise me."

"Ms. Lopez? Can I speak with you?" Lomack said firmly.

"Promise me." Blanche didn't let go of my arm; instead, she squeezed it.

"Alright, I promise — for now."

She released my arm, and I hurried to answer the door.

But how could I keep this from Deputy Lomack? There's currently a potential murder weapon in my bag! A large knife with blood on it! And now, possibly, my blood was on it.

This did not look good... not one bit.

Butterscotch must have sensed my anxiety as she accompanied me to the door. Carefully, I opened it, half expecting to be arrested on the spot.

"Deputy Lomack," I whispered. "What are you doing here?"

He stood at my door with his hands on his hips. His eyes fixed on me with an unbreakable gaze. "Ms. Lopez, I'm here about your camera."

"My—my cam—camera?" I asked, stumbling over my words in surprise. I was sure he was here to arrest me for murder! But he wanted my camera? "You need my camera?"

"Yes," he said with a nod. "But I'll take your memory card."

"You can't have her memory card!" Blanche yelled behind me, causing me to jump in surprise. "That's private property."

"It's part of my crime scene. She may have taken photos important to this case."

"It's not Birdie's job to solve this crime — it's yours!" Blanche pushed past me in determination.

They leaned towards each other, both refusing to yield. "I'll have you arrested for obstruction—"

Blanche pointed at him. "Obstruction of justice! You've

thrown those words around so much they don't scare me anymore."

"Now see here—"

"Wait!" I shouted as I stepped between them, a hand going to each chest to keep them apart. "Here, it's yours." I handed him the memory card — never had I moved so fast. I had run to where Blanche had stashed my camera bag and was back within moments. "You can keep it."

"Birdie," Blanche said in disgust. "You know how important those photos are to me."

"This is important, too," I remarked before refocusing on Lomack. "Deputy Lomack, I hope that's all you need here."

He calmly took the flash drive and gave me a smile and a nod; he had a rather friendly smile. My heart beat against my chest, and I was thankful he was leaving. I wanted him off my porch and far away. Did Blanche forget what was in my camera bag?

"Goodbye," he said before leaving.

I turned back to Blanche and pushed her into the house. The look of pure hatred for me was clear.

"How could you?" she accused. "You knew how much I needed those photos and gave them to him?"

I nodded. "Yes, but he would not leave here without them—"

"Birdie—"

"I only gave him a copy."

"A what?" she asked, confused. "A copy? How did you make a copy so fast?"

"I didn't. I always shoot with a backup memory card in case one of them becomes corrupted. It's saved my life more than once."

"What?" The tension from her face eased, and her shoulders relaxed as the fight she had worked up deflated. "What are you waiting for? Get those photos uploaded before he comes back!"

A knock sounded once more at my door.

"Don't you dare open it," Blanche snapped. "It could be Lomack!"

The person on the other side of my door wasn't Lomack. I could see the familiar outline of my neighbor Mason Whisky Moon through the stained glass window.

Chapter Four

"Mason, what are you doing here?" I asked. Butterscotch stood at my side, her tail wagging in excitement.

"I saw Lomack and wondered what had happened," he explained. "Did something happen in your aunt's case?"

He was asking about the events from the night before when we had discovered that my neighbor, Jack Moss, had murdered my aunt over a dispute about feeding the peacocks.

"No," I said as I shook my head. "He was here about another case," I gestured for him to enter, and he followed me into the kitchen. "Would you like some coffee? You might as well hear it from us because it will be all over town."

"Mason Whisky Moon," Blanche shouted his full name in surprise. "What are you doing here at this hour?" She glanced at her watch and raised her eyebrows. "Or are you coming back from somewhere dubious?"

"Blanche, he's not a suspect," I reassured her. "He's my next-door neighbor."

"I don't know. Considering what happened with Jack Moss, I wouldn't make assumptions about your next-door neighbors not being murderers.

"If it makes you feel any better, I have an alibi," Mason stated with a smile.

I poured him a cup of instant coffee. "It's not my best coffee, but it's hot," I said.

"Where were you coming from?" Blanche inquired, arching an eyebrow.

"I was at the distillery all night," Mason calmly explained.

Moon Distillery, owned by Mason, was a legacy started by his great, great, great grandfather, Whisky Moon, a bootlegger who ran an illegal whisky business during prohibition.

"Overseeing production," he added, taking a long sip of the coffee. "Twenty people were part of the crew I was with. You're welcome to come and talk to any of them." He placed the cup on the island and studied each of us carefully. "Does this have anything to do with the body found at the marina?"

"What?" I asked, surprised, spitting out my coffee. "How do you know about that?"

"I heard it on my police scanner," he explained.

"What are you doing with one of those?" I asked, intrigued.

He shrugged as though it was customary to have one on hand. "It was my great grandfathers."

"Then you should know why Lomack was here," Blanche said with a smile.

"I better upload those photos for you, Blanche," I said, grabbing the laptop and getting started.

She came over to my side to look over my shoulder. Mason took the other side and observed as I worked.

I sensed there was more he wasn't sharing about his visit. Maybe he didn't want to say anything around Blanche. I couldn't fault him for that; she had just interrogated the man!

It was an hour before Blanche, and I finished the article. She headed to the office to oversee the printer.

"Why don't we grab breakfast?" Mason asked. "I know a place nearby."

I wanted to take him up on the offer, but I needed to take Butterscotch for a walk. "That sounds like a great idea, but Butterscotch needs to go out."

Mason picked up the leash and called for her. "I'll come with you. There's something I need to discuss with you."

"What is it?" My earlier hunch had been correct. He had something to say, but not in front of Blanche.

Mason held the door open.

"Don't keep me in suspense," I said.

He waited as I locked the door and leaned in close. "I kept quiet about it in front of Blanche, but Moon's News is up for sale."

I dropped the keys out of my hand. Mason caught them smoothly.

"What did you just say?" I asked. "Did you just say Moon's News is for sale?"

Butterscotch began jumping at my feet; she wanted to get moving.

"Her father is selling the newspaper," he explained.

We headed down the porch steps with Butterscotch leading the way. It was after six a.m., but it felt much later. It had been quite the morning.

"How do you know this?"

"I heard it from Henry Pruitt, who asked me if I was interested in buying it."

I stopped, but Butterscotch kept going and nearly took my arm with her. I stumbled over my feet as I fought to keep up with her. Mason saw me struggle and took the leash.

"I got it," he said.

"Blanche doesn't know this," I whispered, afraid of being overheard. However, looking around, it didn't look like anyone else was on the street. "She doesn't know her father is selling the paper."

"He asked me not to tell anyone." His eyes moved away from me, and he looked a bit sheepish with the confession.

"So why did you tell me this?" I asked.

"She's your friend," he said quietly. "I thought you'd want to tell her what was happening so she would have a chance to buy it herself."

I shook my head. "How do I tell my best friend her father is selling the paper she's working so hard to save?"

"Tell her quick. I'm not the only one he's approached about this."

"Did he say why he's selling?"

Mason shook his head.

But I knew the answer...

Chapter Five

Freshly dressed in a vintage burgundy tea-length linen dress adorned with large red buttons, Mason and I strolled into *Sweeties Lattes*, the coffee shop owned by Lindsay Zimmer.

The coffee shop buzzed with activity as customers kick-started their day. Lindsay was at the front counter, greeting customers and taking orders. Her face fell as she spotted us approaching. She quickly rubbed her eyes with the back of her hands and rested them on either side of the terminal. "What can I get you this morning?" she asked with a forced smile.

"Are you alright?" I asked, concern evident in my voice.

She glanced at me briefly before redirecting her gaze to the tablet. "Just swamped with the morning rush, but I'm fine. What can I get you?"

Her eyes were red, as though she'd been crying, and her face was flushed. Deciding not to press her further, I gave her my order. "I'll have a hot Chai Latte with oat milk and pumpkin."

She nodded, turned to Mason, and asked, "And for you?"

"I'll have the same," Mason replied.

As Mason paid, I spotted Doris Gilbert walking through the door with a massive smile on her face, kind of like the cat who ate the canary. Known for her town gossip blog, wherever Doris went, tales followed. She immediately spotted us at the counter and gave us a wave as she called out my name.

"Brace yourself," I whispered to Mason. "Doris Gilbert is headed our way."

"Birdie Lopez!" Doris exclaimed. "It's about time I ran into you — and with Mason Whisky Moon. How perfect is this?" She positioned herself to block us from leaving the counter but leaned over my shoulder as she spoke with Lindsay. "I'll have an iced decaf with sweetener. But not too much ice, and please be heavy-handed with the sweetener, dear."

"Excuse us," Mason said as we attempted to step past her.

"Of course," Doris replied but held out her hand to stop us from moving. "But did you hear what happened at the marina this morning?" Her gaze fixed on me.

A chill ran down my spine. Did Doris know I had been at the marina earlier? I bit my bottom lip as I considered the possibility.

Mason wasted no time in responding, "A body was discovered at the marina."

"Oh, so you had heard about that." A look of disappointment clouded Doris's round face. Her jaw clenched and unclenched as she pondered Mason's reply. "I had just been to the Sheriff's Station," she stated as she clasped her hands at her waist. "I was informed that a statement will be released shortly. But I did hear from my source at the station that it was Nick Baker they found tied up in a lobster net! Nick Baker!"

Lindsay gasped as she stepped out from behind the counter, her eyes wide. "What about Nick?"

Doris took her notebook from her purse and flipped through the pages, a pen ready. "The deputies found the body of Nick Baker entangled in a lobster net. Weren't you friendly with the man?"

"Nick?" Lindsay's brow furrowed as she whispered his name. "He's... he's gone?" Her eyes softened, and a faint smile played on her lips. She must have processed the question Doris had asked her as she quickly stated firmly, "No, no, I wasn't friends with him."

The door to the cafe opened, and Jeremy Jones hustled inside, hurrying to the counter. "I'm picking up my mobile order," he rushed out of breath.

Lindsay nodded and retrieved a brown bag, which she promptly handed to Jeremy, who eyed me curiously.

Jeremy pointed at me with his cell phone. "You know we still got your aunt's car at the shop."

I had forgotten all about her car. I had instructed Peter Hayes to sell it for me because I had no use for it. After all, I didn't drive. I preferred getting around town on my bicycle. "How do you know about my car?" I asked. As far as I knew, he didn't work with Peter, so I found it odd that he asked me about it.

Doris was quick to answer. "Jeremy works with Peter Hayes — he's a mechanic."

My phone chimed with a notification, and I quickly retrieved it from my purse. Blanche had sent me a link to the article she had written about Nick's case. It prominently featured my photos.

"What is it?" Mason inquired.

I showed him my phone. Just then, the door to *Sweetie's Latte's* swung open, revealing Lois Jones, the head of the H.O.A. Her gaze fixed on me with determination, and without hesitation, she headed straight towards me.

I caught a flash of Jeremy as he exited via the back door. Why did it appear he was avoiding his mother?

"Just the person I was hoping to find," Lois declared.

"Well, hello, Lois," Doris said, her face lighting up. "Are you looking for me?"

Lois didn't spare Doris a glance — her focus was laser-like on me. "I've received several complaints about your yard."

"My yard?" I questioned, baffled. What could this be about? "Complaints about what?"

Lois didn't keep me waiting. "Your fence needs maintenance. There are parts of it that need to be painted."

"What?" She couldn't be serious.

"You must fix it by Friday or face hefty fines."

Doris's head snapped towards me so swiftly that I was sure she must have strained her neck at the sharp movement. "Wow," she gasped. "Can I get a comment for my blog?" she asked, pen and paper still in hand.

"No," I stated firmly before returning my attention to Lois. "Who complained about my fence?"

Lois smiled, crossing her arms. We were now the center of attention in the cafe. "I'm not obliged to disclose that information to you." She glanced at Mason and then back at me. "Enjoy your day." With that, she turned and left with a lighter step.

"How did she even know I was here?" I wondered aloud.

Lindsay brought our drinks over and held them out to us. "That woman has eyes all over the H.O.A." She rested her hands on her hips as she watched Lois through the window. "There's nothing she doesn't know."

"You know her well?" I asked. Did Lindsay know something about Lois? And why did she seem relieved when she heard it was Nick Baker's body found at the Marina?

"Well enough," she replied with an easy smile before greeting the next customer.

Chapter Six

SHORTLY AFTER RETURNING HOME, A KNOCK ECHOED at my front door. I glimpsed a hunched figure through the stained-glass window.

Butterscotch stood beside me as I opened the door to find Jeremy Jones. He had his hand raised, ready to knock again. Stepping back, he smoothed down his button-up shirt. "Hi," he boomed. "How are you?"

"Hi," I greeted, awaiting an explanation for his unexpected visit.

Jeremy seemed unhurried, smiling and tucking his hands into his pockets.

"Can I help you?" I inquired.

"Maybe," he replied, a grin playing on his face. "I saw you with Blanche at the marina this morning."

"You were at the marina?" I asked with surprise. What was he doing there?

He cast a glance over his shoulder and then back at me. "Can I come inside? I'd rather not discuss this out here."

"Yes, of course, come in." I stepped aside, gesturing for him to enter. Butterscotch barked and nuzzled his hand, but he pulled back, looking at her with concern. "Do you like dogs?" I asked.

"Hi, there," he said to Butterscotch with concern. "I've never had one." His words strained.

"You've never had a dog?" I called Butterscotch over and directed her to her doggy bed, where she had her toys. "So, what brings you over?"

Jeremy stood stone-still in the entryway of the living room. "I saw you at the docks," he explained. "Taking pictures."

The way he said, 'taking pictures,' made me uncomfortable. "Are you worried I took your photo?" I asked, surprised that I hadn't noticed him. I hadn't reviewed all of my photos. Perhaps he was in a couple of them. Was that why he had come by?

"Why would I be worried about that?" He asked, frowning. He ran a hand through his hair and fiddled with his metal watchband. "I wanted..." he murmured, glancing over his shoulder.

An icy shiver ran down my spine, and I couldn't help but shudder. "What did you want?" I asked, prompting him to continue, feeling a growing sense of unease.

He cleared his throat. "My boss, Peter Hayes, sent me to talk to you about your Aunt Lula's car."

"Oh." But why come here instead of just making a phone call?

"Peter wants you to come by and sign the papers. He found a buyer." He re-pocketed his hands and leaned back on his feet.

The ringing of my cell phone startled him, causing him to jump.

I winced inwardly. "Hold on," I said as I turned to retrieve my phone.

"It's okay. I got to get back to work." His eyes locked with mine, and for a moment, I thought he needed to share something important with me. He opened his mouth to speak but promptly closed it before spinning around and heading quickly out the door.

"Jeremy!" I called from the top step of my porch, but he was already on the street, jumping into his car.

My phone was still ringing. I reached for my purse, which sat on an oversized chair by the fireplace. After rifling through my bag, I found my phone, only to see I had missed Blanche's call. Within moments, I received two text messages from her.

I need to speak with you.

I'm on my way. See you soon!

True to her word, Blanche arrived at my home shortly after she had sent the text. I had the door open for her before she could knock.

"Birdie," she greeted, her voice brimming with excitement. "Our article went national!"

"What?" I asked, surprised by the news. "Really?"

Blanche had a bag of takeout in her hand. "I brought Italian," she said, pushing past me as she headed into the kitchen. "But I can't stay long; I need to see Dad and tell him the news in person."

"With news like this, I would have thought you'd gone straight there," I remarked, following her into the kitchen.

Blanche's phone vibrated. She pulled it out of her pocket and rolled her eyes at the name on the screen.

"Who's that?" I asked as she sent the caller to voicemail.

She sighed. "Lomack."

"Deputy Lomack?" I asked, concerned. "Why would he be calling you?"

"I don't know," she said sheepishly. "I've been avoiding his calls."

"Blanche," I gasped. "It could be important."

She shrugged as she began unpacking the trays from the bag. "I think I know why he's calling."

I thought of the knife — the potential murder weapon I had hidden in my pantry. "We need to do something about that knife!"

A knock at my door diverted my attention, and I rushed to answer it. "Mason," I said as I opened the door.

"Birdie," his voice tense. "I just heard on the police scanner that Lomack is coming here."

"Here?" I gasped. "Why is he coming here?"

He held up his phone, displaying the article on Moon's News I had shown him earlier. "It's about this," he said. "Your photos."

I took his phone from his hands. Despite having read the article, I glanced at it as if expecting to find something new.

"He's upset about the photos?" My heart sank. I should've known better than to post them. But I was helping Blanche. I bit my lip and handed Mason back his phone. "Thanks for the heads-up."

He followed me into the kitchen, where we found Blanche holding a plate and fork.

"What's happening?" she asked, mouth full of food.

"Lomack's on his way over to talk to us about the photos," I explained, feeling a sense of dread. I wanted to give Lomack the knife, but by doing so, I would look guilty of murder. I can see it now. I'll hand over the weapon, and next, I'll be sitting in a jail cell.

I need to find out who planted that knife in my bag. It had to have been that man in the grey hoodie. He must have dropped it in there when he shoulder-checked me...

A knock echoed at the door, causing me to jump and

Butterscotch to bark; her tone was loud and deep. I peeked out of the kitchen to look through the stained glass. I could see Lomack's silhouette.

"He's here," I announced, moving towards the door. I took a deep breath, forcing a smile before answering. "Hello, Deputy Lomack," I greeted, my voice steady.

"What were the two of you thinking?" He demanded, his voice sharp. "You were supposed to give me all your photos on this case."

"But we did," Blanche protested as she approached the door. "There was nothing wrong with using the duplicates."

"It would have been a professional courtesy not to, Ms. Pruitt." Lomack's hands rested on his belt as he leaned towards her. "What were you thinking?"

She started to speak but seemed to change her mind, retreating into the kitchen for safety.

"I'm sorry about this," I apologized to Lomack. "We posted nothing that would jeopardize the case."

Lomack's gaze bore into me as he pointed but quickly dropped his hand, a look of defeat on his face. "There's nothing to be done about it now. Next time you want to post photos about this case, check with me first."

He turned to leave; a sharp curse muttered under his breath as he rushed down the porch steps to his patrol car. Closing the door behind him, I leaned against it in relief, glad the confrontation was over.

Blanche peeked out of the kitchen with her purse and car keys. "Is he gone? I hate to leave like this, but I must head back to the office."

"Why?" I asked, opening the door for her. "What are you going to do?"

She clutched the keys tightly; they would surely leave an impression on her palm. "I need to solve this murder. Just think what it would do for the paper if I can solve this." She muttered to herself, rather than addressing me or Mason.

"You want to solve his murder?" Mason inquired.

Blanche nodded. "Yes." Her gaze locked onto mine, and I was sure I could read her thoughts.

"*We* have to solve this case," I said.

I didn't want to tell Mason about the potential murder weapon hidden in my house. *Who might try to frame me, and when would they inform Deputy Lomack about it?* "But we don't know where to start," I said, though I thought about Jeremy Jones. Why was he here, and what did he want to talk to me about?

"I'll call you in an hour," Blanche said as she hurried out the door. "I have an idea."

"Wait! What's your idea?" I asked, following her out onto the porch.

"You'll see. I can't explain it now." Blanche didn't stop; she hurried down the path to her car.

"I'm not sure I'm going to like her plan," I said. "She dives in without considering the consequences."

Mason stood at my side. "Does she know?"

"Are you asking if I told her about the impending newspaper sale?" I asked. "No, I haven't told her about it." I leaned against the rail post. I suddenly wanted a cigarette.

"Will you tell her about the sale?" He asked.

I shook my head; how could I tell her? It would surely break her heart. Was I the right person for the task? Shouldn't it come from her father? "She should hear it from her dad," I said as I glanced at him. "But... are you going to buy it?"

"It would be a charity case if I did; it's losing money."

"But that's why she's doing everything possible to engage readership. She's trying to save it."

Butterscotch barked at us from the open door. It was her

way of reminding me it was time for our walk. The walk would be a delightful distraction. Or so I thought...

Chapter Seven

Butterscotch and I set out for our afternoon walk, and all I could think about was this revelation about Moon's News. Would Mason decide to buy it? Should I tell Blanche about the sale?

Butterscotch pulled me towards a bush, and suddenly, a peacock jumped out of it, screeching at us in protest.

"Butterscotch," I shouted as she tried to chase after it. "No!" I pulled at her leash, urging her to follow me down the sidewalk. "Leave the peacock alone."

"Is everything okay?" Lindsay asked, perched at the top of her porch, tying her shoelaces.

"Yes," I nearly shouted in surprise; she caught me off guard. "Are you going out on a run?" I asked, reasonably sure of the answer, as she was dressed in yoga pants and a fitted shirt.

She planted her feet on either side, turning her waist back and forth in a stretch before heading down the porch steps. "I run about four miles every day."

As she approached, I noticed her eyes were red, and once again, it looked like she had been crying. She appeared distracted as she glanced back at the door behind her as though she were looking for someone.

The door suddenly creaked open. Her husband David clutched a suitcase in one hand and his car keys in the other. The door slammed shut behind him.

"What are you doing?" Lindsay asked, her voice squeaked.

"I'm not staying here," he grumbled as he made his way to his car parked in the driveway. "I'll have my brother pick up the rest of my stuff."

"You don't have to go," she pleaded, following him to the car. "We can talk about this."

He tossed his suitcase in the back seat before turning to her. "There's nothing to talk about." His gaze shifted to me; he blushed, startled to find me gawking, and hurried into the car.

Lindsay smacked her hand against the window. "We need to talk about this," she cried. "Please don't go."

Butterscotch and I stood by her side as we watched him drive away.

"Are you all right?" I asked. "Where is David going?"

She folded her arms across her chest and lowered her head. "He's leaving me."

"What?" Why would he do that? They had just gotten married! "Can I do anything for you?" I touched her shoulder. I hesitated to intrude, but I couldn't abandon her.

Her shoulders shook, and she cried; before I knew it, she turned to me and cried on my shoulder. Butterscotch barked, worried.

"Can I get you something?" I asked. "Can I call someone?"

She pulled back from me. "This is all Nick Baker's fault," Lindsay shouted as she turned to run back up the steps. The door to her home slammed shut behind her.

"Nick Baker?" I asked, confused. "What does Nick have to do with this?"

Butterscotch began tugging at her leash, telling me she wanted to keep going. "Okay, okay," I said to her before moving down the street to continue our walk.

But I couldn't stop thinking about what had just happened. What was Nick's involvement with Lindsay and David? I must talk to Blanche; she knew Lindsay — they're old friends. She might be able to shed light on the situation.

After about an hour on our walk, Butterscotch and I returned home only to find Lindsay waiting on our porch.

"Lindsay, are you all right?" I asked. She looked like she had run a 5K in under five minutes, sweating and panting, and her ponytail was a mess.

She met us on the bottom step. "I need to talk to you. Do you gotta minute?"

"Yes." I dug the key from my pocket and unlocked the door. Butterscotch dashed in, leading the way. "Can I get you something to drink? I can make us some tea. I have chamomile."

She shook her head. "Can I have a glass of water?" she asked as she followed me into the kitchen and sat at the island table. "I didn't know where else to go. You were the last person I saw tonight — so I thought of you."

I poured her a glass of cold water from a pitcher I kept in the fridge. She didn't waste a second before downing it.

"What happened?" I asked. "What was that all about with David?" I've known Lindsay from the summers I'd spent with my Aunt Lula. But as time passed, we had grown apart. So, I don't see the dynamic between her and her husband.

"I need your help," she said as she poured herself another glass.

"With what?" I asked. I sat across from her and tried to

wait patiently. Butterscotch nuzzled my hand before heading out through the doggy door.

"With Lois Jones."

That had caught me off guard. I had heard her argue with her husband about Nick Baker. So, what was Lois Jones' involvement in this?

"Lois Jones?" I asked as she took a long sip of water. "How is she involved with you and David?"

"She's the reason my marriage is falling apart," she shouted. Lindsay coughed and smacked her chest a few times with her hand as she tried to dislodge the water caught in her throat.

"Are you all right?" I asked, worried she was choking.

She waved me off as she said she was okay. "You're working for Moon's News, right? What if I gave you a tip about Lois? Can you write an article about her without naming me a source?"

"I don't write articles; I take photos for the paper."

Lindsay grew quiet; she placed her elbows on the tabletop and rested her head on her hand. "Lois is a tyrant around here. Someone has to stop her."

"Stop her from what?" I asked, trying to get back on track.

She sat up and looked at me as though I were mad. "Ruining everything," she shouted. "Lois has the sheriff in her pocket. He lives in our H.O.A. If he wants special privileges, he has to go to Lois for them." Lindsay stood. "She keeps files on everything locked in her home office. And she has a file on everyone."

Lindsay leaned close and placed her hand firmly on my shoulder. "It's only a matter of time before she comes after you," she whispered. "Especially after what your Aunt Lula did to her."

"My Aunt Lula?" I asked. "What did she do to Lois?"

She gasped. "You don't know?"

Her words caused me to shiver. Lindsay leaned away as she looked at her watch.

"What did my Aunt Lula do?" I asked again.

Her eyes settled back on me but seemed far away. "Your aunt was talking to an attorney — one who is not from Moon's Landing."

"Why would my aunt do that?" I asked, but she must have read the doubt in my eyes.

"You don't have to believe me about any of this, but you'll wish you had in time." Lindsay placed the glass in the sink and left my house without another word.

Chapter Eight

I took a taxi to see Peter Hayes as I had decided it was best to speak with him in person. I wanted to talk to him about his employee, Jeremy Jones.

When I found him, he was in his office on a phone call, which he quickly ended as he spotted me standing in the doorway.

"Birdie," he stood and leaned over the cluttered desk to shake my hand. "Don't tell me — you're here about your aunt's car."

"Yes. Jeremy told me you found a buyer."

"I did, I did. I have the paperwork here." He began moving stacks of paper around his desk as he searched.

An angry voice coming from the waiting room drew both of our attention. "I'm not going to pay that! That's extortion!"

I moved aside as Peter flew past me to discover what was happening. "I'll be right back," he assured before racing down the short hall and into the waiting room. "What's going on here?" I heard him yell.

Left in his office, I thought I'd save time and look for the pink slip myself. I circled the desk and began searching. Sure enough, the title was buried underneath a stack of folders.

A receipt slipped out as I moved a folder. Written in black ink was the name JONES. The sheet was stapled to an invoice initialed with LJ and paid from an account from Cornerstone Properties.

Cornerstone is the firm that handles the H.O.A.'s accounts. Why is this invoice paid with H.O.A. funds?

"Birdie," Jeremy stood at the door, watching me intently.

I stuffed the sheets into a file and spun around to face Jeremy. My heart was racing from possibly being caught rifling through Peter's desk.

Jeremy glanced behind him and pointed down the hallway, and I spotted a camera pointing directly into this office. "Peter sent me back here to retrieve the pink slip for you to sign... I've got the check for you right here." He took a step inside.

"Oh," I gasped. "I found it." I quickly stepped back and knocked a black gym bag off a chair.

Jeremy handed me a pen. "Just sign here."

I quickly signed and handed the pen and title back to him. "Here you go."

"Funny thing," Jeremy said as he held onto the pen. "Your aunt was sure that car was a lemon. She brought that car here multiple times in the last few months."

"She did?" I asked, more out of politeness than curiosity. "Well, I need to get going." I stuffed the check into my purse and left.

* * *

As I returned home, I saw a note taped to the door. I stood still as I blankly stared at it.

Who left this here? I glanced around but didn't see anyone. I reached for the note and reread it.

They are coming for you.

Run.

I nearly dropped the note. Carefully, I re-examined it. I recognized this paper! It was the same type of yellow paper as the last note I had received, the one suggesting my aunt's death was no accident.

My cell phone began ringing, jolting me out of my daze. "Hello?" I whispered into my phone.

"Birdie?" Blanche's voice helped me relax. "You won't believe what just happened."

"You won't believe what I'm looking at," I countered.

"Birdie, it's Lindsay Zimmer!" She rushed her words so quickly that she sounded breathless. "She was in an accident."

"An accident?" I asked, confused. "Is she alright?"

"She was run off the road."

I nearly dropped my phone. "Who would do that to her?"

Police sirens wailed behind me. The blues and reds from their lights reflected onto my home. I turned to face the approaching cars, wondering what was happening now.

"Blanche," I whispered. "The police are here."

"What?" her voice rose. "What are they doing there?"

The patrol cars skidded to a stop in front of my house. Lomack was the first to exit his vehicle. His face showed clear disappointment.

"I have to go. I think I'm in trouble."

"I'm on my way." Blanche disconnected the call.

Lomack walked right up to me, holding a piece of paper firmly in his hand, which he handed me. "We have a warrant to search your home and garage."

"What? Why?"

"You're in a lot of trouble, Birdie."

A deputy headed into the garage, breaking the lock on the door as they gained access. "What is this about?" I asked Lomack.

"You better call a lawyer," he said firmly. He placed the warrant in my hand before heading into the garage.

A steady stream of my neighbors began making their way into my yard. Some were talking on their phones, and others were taking photos of the police.

I spotted Mason rushing past a deputy who began directing my neighbors away from my house.

"I heard what was happening," he said. "Are you all right?"

My eyes were on the garage door. *Why are they in there?*

I turned to Mason, feeling defeated. I should have turned that knife over when I had the chance. "I'm going to need you to take care of Butterscotch." It was only a matter of time before they searched my house and found that knife hidden in my pantry.

Lomack emerged from the garage with a black bag in his hand. "Ms. Birdie Lopez," he hurried over to me. He wouldn't even look at me. "You have the right to remain silent," he said as he read me my rights.

"What is that?" I asked as I pointed at the black gym bag in his hand. I had never seen it before — wait, I had... I had seen—

"This belonged to Nick Butler," Lomack said gravely.

"No, that bag belongs to Peter Hayes!"

"That's not possible. It has Nick Butler's I.D. inside."

I felt a pair of handcuffs clip onto my wrists. Mason assured me he'd post my bail and get me out of jail.

When would they discover the knife? The possible murder weapon?

Suddenly, I found myself in the back of a patrol car with

the door ajar. Somehow, Lois Jones crossed to me. She leaned down; her hand rested on the car's roof as she peered at me. A smile played on her lips. She didn't say a word as she forcefully closed the door as if imprisoning me.

Perhaps she was.

I'VE BEEN HELD IN AN INTERROGATION ROOM ONCE before, back when I had been arrested in Los Angeles, but thinking back on it, Los Angeles felt like ages ago.

I sat alone. My hands were no longer handcuffed, and I rested them on my lap. Lomack's departure filled me with dread, convinced he would return with my impending doom.

I know that bag had been the one I had seen in Peter's office, but how did it get into my garage so fast? I had just left his office, granted it took a while for my taxi to pick me up. The driver said it was a busy evening and apologized for the wait.

The door opened, and Blanche raced in her face flush. "Birdie, don't worry. It's going to be fine."

I wasn't sure I believed her, but I played along because I could see she was about to burst into tears.

"What are they saying?" I asked. "How did they find that bag in my garage, and what about—"

Blanche raised her hands to my mouth. "Say nothing! They are listening." She pointed at the two-way mirror.

I clamped my mouth shut and fastened my hands together out of nervousness.

The door opened, and Lomack entered with a file in hand. One glance at it revealed my name on it. "What are you doing in here?" He snapped at Blanche. "Get out, or I'll have you arrested." He opened the door and shouted for Deputy Joe Murphy.

"I'm staying with her," Blanche proclaimed as she took my hand.

Lomack looked sharply at her. "You're not her legal counsel."

"I went to law school," she said as she raised her chin. She added under her breath, "For a year." Blanche had attended law school and hated every moment.

Deputy Joe arrived at the door. "Sir?" He asked Lomack. "What do you need?"

Lomack's eyes were firmly on Blanche. "Have a seat," he said, pointing at her.

"Um, excuse me, sir?" Deputy Joe stepped farther into the room.

Lomack turned sharply at him. "What is it?" He snapped. "Can't you see I'm busy?"

He cleared his throat. "Mason Whisky Moon is outside. He says he needs to speak to you right now."

"Why do I care what Mason Moon wants?" His voice rose with each word. "Do I look like I care what Moon wants?"

Joe flushed, uncomfortable, and tugged at his tie. "He said he's not leaving until you come out and speak with him."

Lomack slammed my file on the table and pushed past Joe. "Wait until I get..."

Joe stayed in the room with us. His face relaxed with each passing second. He looked firmly at me and said, "You're in a lot of trouble, Birdie."

Joe Murphy, a young deputy somewhere in his late twenties, had been so kind to me when I was investigating my Aunt Lula's murder. He had let me sneak a look at her case file.

"What does Mason want to talk to Lomack about?" I asked, hoping he could tell me.

Blanche reached for the file Lomack had left behind. She quickly scanned it. "Lomack is building a case against you." Her eyes were sharp on me in disbelief. "You are the prime suspect!" She removed a photo from the file and placed it before me. "That's your earring."

"You're not supposed to touch that." Joe took the file and photo from her and placed them exactly where Lomack had left it. He glanced back at the closed door. "He can come back any second."

"But he knows I was at the crime scene that morning," I argued. I wanted to read the file to see what it said about me. "Joe, let me read it."

Blanche reached for it again. She and Joe had a tug-of-war over it, and Blanche won. Joe leaned against the door. He urged her to be quick.

"There's a witness," she gasped.

"A witness?" I stood up and leaned over her shoulder to read the file. "The name is not listed."

Joe grabbed the file out of Blanche's hand. "I hear him coming back," he whispered. He had the file in his hands as Lomoack entered the room.

"What's going on in here?" Lomack asked as he eyed us one by one. He noticed the file in Joe's hand and took it from him. "Give me that!"

"If you need nothing else," Joe said before quickly leaving us.

Lomack pointed the file directly at me. "What's your relationship with Mason Moon?" He asked.

"Mason?"

"Why would he go to all the trouble of calling up Judge Samson to get you out of here?"

Blanche stepped in front of me and crossed her arms. "So what you're saying is Birdie's free to go."

"For now!" He opened the door, swinging it open for us. "Don't even think about *running*, Ms. Lopez."

Run... that's precisely what that note said I should do. I moved past Lomack but stopped at the door. "You didn't find a note posted to my door, did you?"

"Birdie, let's not bother Lomack about any notes." She pushed me past him. He merely grumbled at us.

Mason stood at the front desk with Butterscotch at his side. She let out a joyful bark in greeting and tried to run over to me, but he held firmly on the leash.

I looked him in the eyes as I approached. "How did you get me released?"

Blanche didn't waste a moment as she ushered me out of the station. "Let's go, we need to talk."

BLANCHE HAD ILLEGALLY PARKED HER CAR IN A RED zone, but no one seemed to notice. Once inside, she started driving, but it was clear that we were not going back to my house.

"Where are we going?" I asked. Butterscotch was in the backseat; she sat forward and nuzzled my shoulder.

"We're going to my office," she glanced in her rearview mirror. "It doesn't look like we are being followed."

"Why would someone follow us?" I asked, wondering what she knew about this case." I sat back in my seat. "Why was I framed?"

"That's a good question."

It took me a moment to realize this wasn't Blanche's red convertible. This was a grey sedan, and I had never seen it before. "What is with the cloak and dagger?" I asked. "You know something, don't you?"

Blanche pulled into the parking lot of Moon's News. She turned to me, her eyes filled with worry. "This is the safest place I could think of for you," she stated as she parked. "I'm worried about you."

She's worried about me? I'm concerned about her. There's something she hasn't told me yet. Whenever Blanche kept something from me, she tensed up and became quiet. On the ride over, she hardly said one word to me.

"What's happening?" I asked. "What do you know that I don't."

"My father is selling Moon's News. I just found out about it."

"He finally told you?" I asked, relieved she knew, sparing me from keeping it a secret.

"How do you know about it?" Blanche's gaze sharpened as she fixed it on me.

"Well, I—" but someone interrupted me when the front door to the newspaper office opened. "Who's that?"

"That's my assistant," she explained as she jumped out of the car. "Beaker."

Blanche handed the keys to Beaker as I helped Butterscotch out of the car. "Here you go," she said with a smile. "And as promised, there's not a single scratch on it."

"I wasn't worried," he said, smiling as he took the keys from her. He turned to me and held out his hand. "I'm Roy Beaker," he said proudly.

"Hi—"

Blanche cut me off before I could say anything more. "He knows who you are. Let's get inside, and you can tell me how you knew about my father selling the paper. Although I think I might already know the answer." She took Butterscotch's leash and handed it to Beaker. Would you mind getting her a drink? I need to speak with Birdie."

Blanche led me through a maze of offices until we got to the one that had her name on it. On her desk sat the murder weapon — the knife! "What is that doing here?"

She picked it up; at least she had it in a poly bag. "I'm sending it to a friend who works in forensics."

Against her wall was a whiteboard filled with photos and names. My photo was on the board, and under it was the word Suspect. Next to my picture was Lois Jones, and beneath her photo was Mastermind.

"What is this about?" I asked. "Why am I a suspect?"

"You are not a suspect." She stood beside me and looked over the whiteboard. "But it certainly looks like you are."

"Why don't you tell me why you brought me here?" I asked. I took a seat at her desk as I waited for an explanation.

"I brought you here to keep you safe; you're in danger," she explained.

"In danger?" I asked, confused. "In danger from who? Lois?"

"I received a note warning me about writing more articles about Nick Baker. Surprisingly, I found a note taped to your door, written in the same style. I think someone is trying to stop us from finding the truth."

"You received a note, too? Where is it?" I wanted to see it for myself.

"Oh, don't worry, you'll see it in my paper's morning edition."

I couldn't believe what she said. "You're publishing the notes? Is that wise?" It suddenly dawned on me why she was doing it, focusing on selling stories, not uncovering the truth. I stood up. "I refuse to be involved with this," I growled, frustrated by her prioritization of profits. "Did you do this to me?" I asked. "Did you make it look like I'm guilty of murder?"

Her jaw dropped. "No," she nearly shouted. "Why would I do that to you?"

I pointed at the board. "You didn't want me to turn over the murder weapon. Will this be the next scoop? What will be your headline?" I reached for the weapon before storming out of her office.

"Wait," she shouted. "Where are you going with that? Are you trying to get yourself arrested?"

"I was already arrested!" I exclaimed, swerving back to her. Butterscotch hurried over to me.

"Hey," Beaker called out in surprise as the leash slipped from his hand.

I pointed at Blanche; I felt so much disappointment — and betrayal. Was all of this about saving her struggling newspaper? "I quit! Find yourself a new photographer." I picked up Butterscotch's leash. "Let's go."

I glanced at the knife in my hand. I couldn't walk around Moon's Landing with this. I'm just a short distance from the distillery. Someone may still be working and would let me use the phone. I didn't have my purse or my house keys — nothing! Blanche took me out of the station so fast that I didn't even retrieve my belongings.

Well, here's to hoping no one finds me walking the streets with a possible murder weapon in my hand. "Let's go, Butterscotch," I said. "Paws crossed we don't get arrested on the way."

Chapter Eleven

Dusk was settling as the gate leading into the distillery opened to allow a car to drive out. Butterscotch and I hurried in before the gate closed. We headed up the steep hill, which seemed isolating, with rows of trees on either side.

Butterscotch led the way up the road, seemingly unfazed by the hike. I couldn't help but glance over my shoulder several times, wary of coyotes or whatever else might be out here.

A pair of car lights approached from behind. We pulled aside on the road, expecting the car to pass, but it didn't. Instead, the car pulled up alongside us.

"Mason," I said with relief, hiding the knife behind my back, still contained in plastic. "I'm so glad to see you."

Confusion filled his eyes as he rolled down the window and asked. "What are the two of you doing here? Can I give you a ride?"

Butterscotch jumped on the driver's door.

"That would be wonderful," I said.

"Why are the two of you out here? Where's Blanche?" he asked. "I thought she would be with you."

Butterscotch and I hurried to the other side of the car to get in. She moved into the back seat. Holding up the knife, I sighed heavily. "I might as well show you this."

"What is that?"

"I believe this might be the murder weapon in Nick Baker's murder."

"How did you get your hands on this?" he asked, eyeing me curiously.

"It found its way into my bag while photographing the crime scene," I said reluctantly. I then explained about the man who had bumped into me that morning and how I discovered it when I returned home.

"Let's get to my office," he said as he sat back and drove the car into the parking garage. After he parked, he reached into the back seat to retrieve a canvas bag. "Here, put that inside this."

With the knife secured, we headed inside the main office building, with Butterscotch leading. "Something tells me she's been here before," I remarked.

"My office is over here," he pointed down a dark hallway. As we moved inside, the office lights turned on. "I'm calling my attorney."

"What will you tell him?"

"Birdie, someone placed that knife in your bag, and we don't know if they used it in Nick's murder, but we need to speak to someone about it."

His office had expansive windows that overlooked a view of the mountains. A wide desk sat in front of the windows. Mason's desk was bare, not a computer or phone in sight.

"There isn't much in here," I remarked as I turned to see the rest of the office; I noticed an old wooden table against a wall that sat what looked like a vintage police scanner. "So that's where you keep it." I wondered if there was a reason he needed to have it, but considering my situation, I thought it was best not to pry.

He opened a mini fridge and removed a bottle of water, which he poured into a coffee cup. "Here you, girl." He held it out to Butterscotch.

I dropped the canvas bag on top of his desk. "Lomack believes it may have been me who did this."

He shook his head. "Lomack doesn't believe it was you."

"They found my earring at the crime scene — but I had a legitimate reason for being there. But Lomack thinks I'm guilty."

"I read a copy of the report. Lomack doesn't believe you're guilty."

"You read the report?" This surprised me. But considering the man had me released from custody with a simple phone call, it didn't surprise me he also had access to my file. "There's something else. Lindsay Zimmer came to see me and told me I needed to investigate Lois Jones. She said my Aunt Lula had contacted an attorney. I believe Lois was using H.O.A. funds—"

Mason reached for the canvas bag, removed the knife, and carefully studied it. After a moment, he placed it back inside and pulled out his phone from his pocket.

But before he could answer, the police scanner turned on. "That's odd," Mason said as he moved to it. "This shouldn't be on."

"This is Deputy Griffins... I'm at the hospital... Lindsay Zimmer is awake..."

"Lindsay's awake!" I hurried over to the scanner to listen. "Can he hear us?" I whispered.

He shook his head. The operator replied quickly to Griffins. "I will pass the information on to Deputy Lomack. He wanted to know when she woke up."

I glanced at Mason. "We need to get to the hospital... I need to speak to her."

Lindsay tried to warn me about Lois; instead, she was the one who got hurt. Was Lois behind her accident? I was beginning to believe Lois Jones was capable of anything.

Chapter Twelve

AFTER DROPPING BUTTERSCOTCH HOME, MASON and I headed to the hospital to check on Lindsay. He waited in the cafeteria while I took the elevator to see her. As I exited the elevator car, I spotted Lindsay's husband. He didn't see me, and I startled him as I said hello.

He glanced up from his phone, nearly dropping it. His eyes were bloodshot, and he was pale. "What?" he asked, confused.

"How's Lindsay?" I asked.

"She's doing fine," he muttered, moving away, busy with his phone.

The door behind him was ajar; I cautiously peeked in to see if it was Lindsay's room. It was, and she was lying in the bed facing the window.

"Hello," I greeted as I knocked on the door.

She didn't turn around.

"How are you feeling?" I asked, but I didn't walk in any further.

"What are you doing here?" She questioned, voice strained.

"I wanted to check on you; I heard a car nearly hit you while you were running. Are you alright?" I asked.

"Is my husband still out there?" Lindsay asked as she turned to me. Her right eye was swelled shut.

"Yes, I saw him walking away to make a phone call. Should I fetch him?"

She leaned into the pillow as she wiped a tear. "He's probably speaking to his mother — she's a divorce lawyer."

I came forward and sat in a chair. "I don't mean to pry into your business, but why would he speak to his mother about a divorce? You'd only just returned from your honeymoon."

"He thinks I'm having an affair..." her words drifted off into a whisper.

"An affair? Are you?" I questioned.

Her head pivoted to me quickly, a spark of anger in her eyes. "No," she snapped.

"I didn't mean to upset you." I bit my lip as I realized I shouldn't have asked such a question. "I spoke with Blanche... she's sure this wasn't an accident."

Lindsay sat up. "Blanche was there."

"She was?" I asked, surprised. *Blanche didn't mention that.*

"She was the first face I saw when I opened my eyes."

"What happened?" I asked.

"I was on a run when a sedan nearly collided with me. It would have hit me if I didn't jump out of the way." She leaned forward and took my hand. "I didn't see who the driver was, but I know Lois was behind it."

"Lois?" I asked. "Why would she want to hurt you?"

She released my hand and rested against the pillow. "I heard you got arrested... I'm sorry... Lois told me that if I didn't tell Lomack that I saw you arguing with Nick, she would arrange for someone to tell my husband about my affair."

"Why would Lois want you to lie?"

She sat up. "Because of what your aunt tried to do to her. Lois has been playing fast and loose with the H.O.A. monies, and your aunt found out."

"How do you know any of this?" I wasn't surprised.

"It started with Jeremy Jones—"

"What are you doing in here?" David stood at the door holding his phone as if it were on speed dial for security.

I quickly stood up. "Hi," I said with a forced smile. "I thought I'd come by and check on Lindsay."

David stood fixed at the door. His eyes were firmly on me as though I were intruding on his privacy.

"David, this is Birdie Lopez. She and I have known each other since childhood."

His eyes remained sharp. "Then why haven't I met her before?" He asked as though he had found Lindsay in another lie.

"She's only just returned to Moon's Landing," she explained.

I walked over and held out my hand. "I'm sorry we had to meet like this."

He didn't take my hand. I dropped it back to my side. "Have you spoken with the Sheriff about what happened?" I asked.

He gave me a scorching look. "I'd like you to leave."

Deputy Lomack stood behind David. He didn't seem all that happy to find me in Lindsay's room. "What are you doing here, Ms. Lopez?"

"Do you know her?" David asked Lomack.

"Yes, she's a murder suspect," he snapped.

Lindsay gasped. "No, you've got that wrong."

"What?" David asked her, confused, and then promptly pointed at me. "I think it's best if you leave."

Deputy Lomack stood aside and nodded at me in agreement. I didn't want to leave. I needed to talk to her about Lois.

Slowly, I gathered my coat and headed for the door. Once there, I turned back to Lindsay. "I'll speak with you later."

David slammed the door in my face. "Pleasant man, you are," I muttered under my breath.

The elevator door opened, and Lois Jones strode out. Her head down as she typed busily on her cell phone, causing her to walk right into me.

"Humph," Lois mumbled as she hastened backward. Her phone fell, hitting the floor.

My hand reached for it before hers. I quickly saw one of my photos from the crime scene displayed on her screen.

"Give me that," she snapped as she snatched the phone from my hand.

We both stood at the same time. Lois stood higher than me, wearing sky-high heels, and I was in my comfy flats.

"What are you doing here?" Lois demanded.

"I was visiting with Lindsay Zimmer."

She peered over my head just as David opened the door. "Are you still here?" He snapped at me.

Lois smirked as she walked by. "By the looks of it, I'd say the visit didn't go well." She walked right into the room. The door closed promptly behind her.

I crept to the door, straining my ears to hear what they said. My ear carefully touched against the panel; I was sure my heart stopped beating as I tried to tune everything else out. I could only make out mumbling. But I heard the distinct voice of Lois Jones, and she didn't sound happy.

I moved away from the door as the elevator chimed. Deputy Griffins strode off the elevator car. He smiled at me and tilted his head in greeting. He didn't stop as he headed for Lindsay's room. I hurried to catch the elevator before it closed. I quickly pushed the button for the first floor.

I wasn't waiting long for the elevator to reach the lobby. But it surprised me to find Peter Hayes waiting for the car.

"Peter," I said in surprise. "What are you doing here?"

His eyes were wide; he was just as surprised to find me here. "I'm here about Lindsay," he mumbled. "We are on the same running team, and I wanted to ensure she wasn't banged up too bad."

I know he was the one who planted that gym bag in my garage. But why? What did he have to gain by framing me for murder?

I spotted Mason standing near the gift shop, casually watching us. He headed over as Peter stepped into the elevator. His hands were busy tossing a pack of Lucky Stripes back and forth.

I turned to Peter as the elevator doors began to close. "You're not missing a gym bag, are you?"

I was sure his face had darkened, but it could have been the poor lighting. "I don't know what you're talking about."

Chapter Thirteen

"Are you sure you want to do this?" Mason asked as he checked his watch.

I made him drive me to the marina to check out my hunch. "I need to find out why Peter and Lois are framing me for murder," I said as I led the way down the dock and to the boat named *Ecstatic*.

The fisherman Blanche spoke to that morning had disembarked from the boat carrying a tool bag.

"Excuse me," I yelled. "Can we speak with you?"

The fisherman turned around, startled. "What can I help you with?"

"What were you doing on that lobster boat?" I questioned. I hadn't expected to find anyone here. "That's a crime scene."

He held up his tools. "Just doing some maintenance," he explained. "I need to ready the boat for tomorrow."

"You're taking the boat out?"

"Yes, now, if you'll excuse me, ma'am," he said, leaving.

"Wait," I called and held out my hand to keep him from moving. "You were here the morning of the murder. Can you tell me if you saw anything unusual? Anyone hanging around the *Ecstatic* who shouldn't have been?"

He shook his head. "I already answered these questions and then some to the deputy."

Mason removed his wallet. "How much is your time worth?" He asked, holding two one-hundred-dollar bills.

The fisherman stepped closer. "I have time, " he said, reaching for the money.

I held my hand over the bills. "Just answer my questions, please."

"What was it you wanted to know?" He asked as he dropped his hand, and I took the money from Mason.

"Do you know who Lois Jones is?" I glanced back at Mason. "Can you take out your phone and show him a picture?"

Mason retrieved his phone, and after a quick minute, he handed the fisherman his phone with a photo of Lois and Jeremy.

The fisherman studied the photo, taking his time before pointing at it. "I don't know the woman but recognize the man beside her."

"Him?" I asked, taking the phone to view the photo. "That's Jeremy Jones..."

The fisherman nodded. "He was here an hour ago. I had to run him off when I found him onboard the *Ecstatic*."

"You said you chased him off?" Mason questioned. "Do you know what he was searching for?"

The fisherman shook his head, a broad smile on his weathered face. "How could I know the answer to that? But I believe I answered all your questions?"

I handed him the money. "You have. Thank you for your time." I turned back to Mason, disappointed. "We have to find out why Jeremy was here," Could Jeremy have been the man in the grey hoodie? Or could it have been Peter?

"I'll drive us over to Lois's. She'll know how we can find Jeremy," Mason said.

"I ran into Lois at the hospital. She was visiting Lindsay."

"She was there?" He questioned, surprised.

"And so was Peter. Peter seems to be everywhere..."

Could Peter know about what I found on his desk? The receipt and invoices? Did my aunt know about them? I need to find out the name of the lawyer she'd hired. I'm sure that lawyer could tell me everything...

Chapter Fourteen

It was well after nine p.m., and as we pulled onto Lois's street, a familiar red convertible parked across from her house caught my eye. "What is Blanche doing here?" I muttered.

She was walking down the path from the front door to her car. She waved us down.

Jumping out of the car, I confronted her. "What are you doing here?" I demanded.

"I'm sure it's for the same reasons you are," she retorted. "Birdie, I'm so sorry about what happened earlier. If you'd let me explain, you'll understand that I'm not trying to frame you for murder."

"You had the knife in your office and the notes—"

"The what in her office?" Mason asked, joining us.

"I was going to have it analyzed by a friend. Do you think I'd trust the Sherrif with it?"

"The fact that you have it only makes me look more guilty," I yelled.

"Birdie, I would never hurt you," She cried back. "I'm only trying to protect you." She held her hands out to me, palms up. "I was scared, and yes, I acted recklessly, and I'm sincerely sorry."

I didn't want to fight with her. Although she's not to blame, her efforts to assist me were terrible. "I'm sorry too — for believing the worst in you." We hugged, and I immediately felt better, realizing my foolishness in thinking Blanche was framing me. Pulling back, I asked, "What are you doing here?"

"I spoke with Lindsay Zimmer on the phone. She's terrified. She said Lois was at the hospital and threatened her if she didn't keep quiet."

"Did she tell you what about?" I asked. *Does Blanche know about my Aunt Lula's part in this?*

Blanche became serious, glancing over her shoulder and lowering her voice. "Lindsay told me how I can get inside the house."

"You're going to break into the house?" Mason asked, intrigued.

"Lindsay told me that Nick confided in her and was afraid for his life after Peter had confronted him."

"But I thought she wasn't friends with Nick?" I recalled her saying so to Doris.

"Well," Blanche said as she continued. "She told me where we would find evidence in Lois's home office."

"I want to hear more of your story," Mason said. "But, considering the neighbors nearby, this is not the place to discuss it."

Blanche gasped in agreement. "You're right. Let's head back here." She led us to a sideyard. "Lindsay gave me instructions on how to get inside. She said she had done it once before." Blanche walked up to a window. "The silent alarm will trigger once I open this window, but don't worry, I have a code. Lois gave it to Lindsay while helping her with her H.O.A. campaign." She turned to Mason. "Give me a boost, and then I'll open the door around the back."

Blanche didn't give us the option to disagree with her plan as she quickly pushed the window open. With Mason's help, Blanche promptly made it through the window.

Mason and I headed for the back, where we met with Blanche.

"What are we looking for?" I asked. "What did Lindsay tell you we'd find?"

The house was well-kept, and everything was tidy. I followed Blanche to the office.

Mason entered the room first, heading for her desk next to the window, lowering the blinds, and flicking a desk light on. Blanche moved to a file cabinet and opened the top drawer.

Since the office was covered, I checked another room to see what I could discover. I quickly climbed the stairs and made my way to the first door on the left. I didn't turn the light on but moved inside towards a side table and opened the drawer. The room had a chair near the window, and clothes were thrown over it. The wall was occupied mainly by a large TV.

I knelt and checked under the bed and found a floor safe. It was locked. I stood up quickly as Mason rushed into the room.

"A car pulled up. We have to leave."

I grabbed his arm. "Wait, I found a floor safe."

His eyes perked up. "Where?"

I pointed under the bed, and he knelt to look at it. "Lucky for us, this isn't a professional one." He removed a pocketknife from his back pocket. In a quick moment, he had the safe open.

"You know how to open a safe with only a pocket knife?" I asked, amazed.

"What are you two doing in here? We have to go!" Blanche asked as she hurried into the room. "Lois is at the front door."

"Do you have a bag?" Mason asked, using the pocket knife

blade to hold up a watch. "I believe this watch belonged to Nick Baker."

"What is Nick's watch doing here?" I asked. "Does this mean Jeremy—"

"No time for questions." Blanche hurried to the window. "We need to leave this house."

Mason stood at the bedroom door. "She's walking up the stairs."

I was afraid to move. I was worried I'd make a sound and alert her we were in this room. A door closed down the hall. Carefully, Mason glanced outside. He signaled it was safe and held the door open for us to leave ahead of him. I had never moved so fast in my life.

Once we made it outside, Blanche held out a tissue and took the watch from Mason.

"Meet me at the Sheriff's Station," Blanche said before running off with the watch.

The second Mason and I were in his car, I asked, "But this watch proves nothing. There can be countless reasons he had the watch. Why are we going to the Sheriff's Station?"

We were pulling away from the curb when he explained, "Blanche found this…" he removed an electronic tablet from his jacket, and after swiping briefly on it, he handed it to me.

"What is this?" I asked as I examined it.

"Press play," he urged.

A video popped up on the tablet screen. Lindsay was inside Lois's house. She was speaking with Lindsay. The video appeared to be home security footage.

"Stop," Lindsay pleaded to Lois. "My husband thinks I'm having an affair!"

Lois sat at her desk with her back to the hidden camera. "You know what it will take to stay out of jail."

"But I have done nothing wrong, you're the one who—"

Lois stood abruptly and walked around her desk to stand

before Lindsay. "You'll plant the evidence I gave you on Birdie Lopez, or you will lose everything, and I'm talking a lot more than just your marriage."

Tires squealed just before a car smashed into ours!

Disoriented, I sat in a haze, waiting for the world to stop spinning. My car door opened, and I was pulled out of the car.

I sat coughing. "What are you doing?"

I glanced around for Mason, but I didn't see him. He must still be in the car. I heard another car screech to a stop. "I've called the police," Blanche yelled.

Jeremy pulled me to my feet and told me to get into his car. I listened.

Where are we going? And why did I get inside his car? Slowly, my head cleared as I realized I was in trouble.

"Where are we going?" I asked him.

"I've been trying to keep you safe," he stammered. "I made a promise to your aunt."

Chapter Fifteen

"WHAT ARE WE DOING HERE?" I ASKED JEREMY AS WE arrived at the marina.

"Get out of the car," he instructed.

I saw the gun in his hand, and I listened.

"Don't try anything," he said as we exited the car. "I don't want to hurt you."

"But What am I doing here?" I asked. "What did you mean about keeping a promise to my aunt?"

He used the gun to point toward the entrance of the marina. "What were you and your friends doing at my house?"

Slowly, I began to move but didn't take my eyes off the gun. "We wanted to talk to your mom. I was told she had evidence to prove it wasn't me who had hurt Nick Baker."

"It would have been easier if I had been able to talk to you when I came to your house. I should have explained everything."

He never disclosed his purpose for being at my house. Had he been there to warn me about his mother's plans? "Tell me now. How is this helping?" I asked.

He shook his head. And gestured to move. "Get going."

I moved, but I suddenly stopped. "Where are we going?"

He lowered the gun. A scowl formed across his face. "I'm trying to help you."

"You say that but haven't explained how any of this will," I stated. Hoping for intervention, I tried to buy time, expecting Lomack or someone to come to help me.

"My mom and Peter were talking about you," he suddenly turned back as a car horn sounded.

"Deputy Lomack is on his way," Blanche shouted as her car pulled to a stop. I didn't see Mason in the car — I hope he's alright!

Jeremy pivoted and pointed the gun directly at Blanche. Without a moment's thought, I pushed his arms away. Surprised, he stepped back and turned to me, gun in hand. *Well, that did nothing!*

I caught sight of Mason, who had come up behind Jeremy.

"Jeremy," I said, keeping him distracted. "Do you know who harmed Nick?"

He lowered the gun and seemed to relax his shoulders. "It's not safe for you here. I'm trying to—"

Mason jumped and tackled Jeremy to the ground. In the shuffle, the gun flew from them.

I hurried to pick it up.

"You don't know what you're doing," Jeremey yelled as Mason secured him.

I pointed the gun at him. I had never held a gun before, and it felt heavy. Blanche ran to my side and took the gun from my shaking hands.

"What is all of this about?" I demanded.

Jeremy laid back against the ground with his hands tied behind his back with a zip tie.

"Who murdered Nick?" I demanded. "Was it you?"

The sound of sirens rang behind us.

"You don't have much time to answer our questions," Blanche instructed. "Was it you or Lois?"

He shook his head. "The one you need to talk to is Peter Hayes... that's all I'll say."

I turned to Blanche. "It was Peter's bag they found in my garage, and he was here that morning we found Nick."

"Peter has a boat nearby." Mason pulled Jeremy to his feet. "Let's go."

The sirens grew closer. "The sheriff is almost here," I alerted. "Shouldn't we wait?"

"It's not far."

* * *

A soft glow emanated from Peter's small, cozy boat, nestled among similar vessels. It proudly displayed the name *Ocean's Gale*. It was white and adorned with a central cabin and a metal rail.

"Peter!" Mason's voice echoed, hand firmly gripping Jeremy's collar. "Get on board," he instructed.

As Jeremy and Mason climbed aboard, Peter emerged from the cabin. "What are you doing here?"

Blanche and I stood on the docks. She positioned herself in front of me, ready to question him. "We all know what Lois instructed you to do."

We didn't. Blanche was bluffing, but would he fall for it?

Peter's gaze shifted to Jeremy. "I don't know what you're talking about. Why is he restrained?"

"It doesn't matter," she said smugly, lifting her shoulder. "Lomack is on his way here. Don't you hear the sirens?"

Time was slipping away, and we lacked solid evidence beyond Nick's watch and a hunch. "You were here that morning," I reminded him. "I saw you... it was you who dropped that knife in my camera bag."

Nick shook his head. "What are you talking about? I was there, you're right, but I know nothing about putting a knife in your bag. Maybe you should tell Lomack about it."

Lomack had finally arrived, along with Deputy Joe. "What is this all about?" He asked. "I got a call that Jeremy Jones forced Birdie into his car after ramming his into Mason's."

"I have no idea what this is about," Peter claimed, hands on hips. "They just showed up here."

I shook my head. "Nick worked for you for years... why would you hurt him?"

"Nick discovered his secret," Jeremy said, breaking free from Mason. "I heard you speaking with him at the garage... you told him to back off, or he would regret it."

"There were papers on your desk," I shouted at him. "Lois Jones's name was on a receipt, and an invoice was paid by—"

"I often wondered how you could keep your business afloat when you didn't have many customers." Blanche held her voice recorder. "What is Lois's role in all of this?"

Peter frowned. "You believe Lois is behind this? I wish she were."

"What happened between you and Nick?" I asked, pleading with him to tell us.

"I told Nick to walk away, to leave it all alone," Peter began. "But he wouldn't listen. He knew what I was cooking the books. He learned he was going to the Lomack!"

He looked over my shoulder at someone behind me. I turned to see who it was. I spotted Sheriff Newbaker standing behind me.

"How was Lois involved?" I asked.

Peter didn't bother to answer the question as he dove overboard and into the water. The splash reached the decks and brushed across my feet.

"Peter," I yelled as I ran to the water's edge to look for a sign of him. The water was pitch black. I couldn't see anything. *Was he going to get away?* "Does anyone see him?"

"Get him out of the water," the sheriff ordered.

Mason and Deputy Lomack jumped in after him, the latter grumbling before taking the plunge. Mason rose in the water with Peter. Deputy Joe hurried over and fished Peter out of the water.

"Birdie," Jeremy stood at my side.

"Why did you bring me here?" I asked him.

"I wanted us to confront Peter together, get him to admit to what he did."

Deputy Joe held out a pair of handcuffs as he approached. "Jeremy Jones, you'll have to come in and answer some questions."

Jeremy nodded. "Birdie," he said before leaving with him. "Your Aunt Lula. She's the one who discovered that Peter was using the garage to launder money. She made him work on her car to have a reason to be there. He became suspicious because she kept finding something wrong with her car and hung around asking questions."

Handcuffed, Peter wrestled away from Lomack as he charged at Jeremy. He knocked Jeremy to the ground. It took both Lomack and Mason to pull Peter away from him.

"That's enough of that," the sheriff shouted. "Get him into the patrol car."

Mason held up a knife. "Look what I found on him."

My eyes must have doubled in size as I gasped at him in surprise. That was the knife I had found in my bag!

"What?" Peter promptly tripped over his feet as he stared at it in surprise.

"Joe," Newbaker shouted. "Get that weapon from Moon and get it down to the lab."

"That's not possible—" Peter stammered. "I left that on you!" He pointed at me. "How did this get back to me?"

Newbaker walked sharply to Peter and whispered close to him. "I'd keep quiet if I were you." He then yelled at Lomack to arrest him for murder.

Mason held the door of the patrol car open and happily slammed it closed once Peter was inside.

"You have to bring Lois in for questioning," I urged Lomack.

"On what? Hearsay?" Lomack said as he shook his head. "Do you have any evidence to suggest she was in cahoots with Hayes on anything you just stated?"

I stammered. No, I didn't. I didn't grab the receipt and invoice I had found on Peter's desk. But I had seen them. "You can ask Jeremy about it. He will confirm my story."

Lomack moved in close and whispered. "You think the kid will turn on his mother?"

"He's not a kid," I said firmly. "And he will do the right thing. He said he was trying to help me."

Lomack shook his head before walking away. I spun to Mason and whispered. "You planted that knife on Peter."

"I knew it had to be either him or Jeremy, and once I saw how this was playing out, I made a move."

I gasped in surprise. "You were going to pin the murder on one of them?" I shook my head. The last time I had seen that knife was back at his office.

"Would you rather it have been you?"

I shook my head. The answer was obvious. Peter had intended that I be blamed. "No one will believe me about Lois's involvement."

Mason nodded. "And they won't. The sheriff will protect her."

Blanche's phone pinged a text notification, gaining our attention and causing her to sigh heavily. "Oh, no... I need to stop by the office."

Before she could finish, her cell phone rang, and she quickly answered. "Beaker, what is it?"

I couldn't help but see her tense as she listened.

"What?" she asked. "Are you serious? Touch nothing — you called the sheriff? Why would you — of course... Beaker!" She swung back to us and shoved her phone into her back pocket. "He hung up on me."

"What happened?" I asked.

"According to Beaker, someone broke into our office and ransacked the place."

"A burglary?" Mason asked.

Blanche nodded. "Beaker called the sheriff. I must get there before he does. Doris won't scoop me out of my story — I heard her in the background!"

Somehow, the three of us piled into Blanche's two-seater and drove to Moon's News as quickly as possible.

What will we find when we arrive? And how will I convince Lomack about Lois Jones?

Thank You!

Dear Reader,

Thank you so much for taking the time to read this story. I know there are countless books out there, and it means the world to me that you chose to spend your time in the world I've created.

Whether you're a longtime fan or this was your first visit, I'm truly grateful for your support. Readers like you keep these characters alive and help cozy mysteries thrive.

If you enjoyed the book, I'd be honored if you left a review or shared it with a friend—it helps more than you know. But most of all, thank you for reading.

Until next time,

Shelley

Continue Your Visit to Moon's Landing

Moon's Landing Cozy Mysteries

Murder by Association

Murder by Marina

Murder by Copy

Murder by Brewery

Murder by Musical

Murder by Christmas

Murder by Almanac

Murder by Nostalgia

Murder by Masquerade

Murder by Mischief

Murder by Mistletoe

Murder by Exposure

Murder by Box Set Books 1-3

* * *

Related to this Series

Welcome to the Neighborhood

The Dastardly Kringles

* * *

Sweetie's Latte Cozy Mystery

The Halloween Jingle

The Valentine Single

The Shamrock Mingle

The Bunny's Last Hop

Red, White, & Boom!

Ghosts, Gags, & Glazed Donuts

Cranberries, Crimes, and Christmas Lights

The Latte Resolution

The Galentine's Crumble

Mothers, Muffins, and Mischief

* * *

The Moonlit Charm Series

The Moonlit Charm

Tides and Secrets

* * *

The Night Nurse

The Lady Who Never Sleeps

* * *

A Foxglove Bay Mystery Series

A Quiet Death in Foxglove Bay

A Lingering Silence in Foxglove Bay

Before You Go!

If you wish to be notified about my next book, sign up for my mailing list at

Shelley's Newsletter! (if reading from the ebook)
or visit
www.shelleyweiss.com

If you'd like to read a free short story about Birdie and Butterscotch as they solve the case of the missing bicycle, you can click here or go to
https://dl.bookfunnel.com/ae0shg99hl

About the Author

Shelley Weiss writes cozy mysteries filled with charm, heart, and loyal canine companions. Based in sunny Southern California, she brings small-town secrets and suspense to life with every turn of the page.

www.ingramcontent.com/pod-product-compliance
Lightning Source LLC
Chambersburg PA
CBHW051251160726
47994CB00003B/1111